Pla

# THE
# SEA TIGER

# Terry Jones

## The Sea
## Tiger

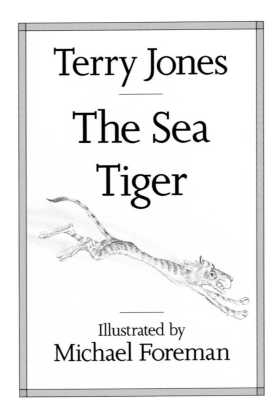

Illustrated by
# Michael Foreman

PAVILION

JF

This edition first published in Great Britain in 1994 by
PAVILION BOOKS LIMITED
26 Upper Ground, London SE1 9PD

Text copyright © Terry Jones 1981
Illustrations copyright © Michael Foreman 1994

The moral right of the author and illustrator has been asserted.

Designed by Bet Ayer

A CIP catalogue record for this book
is available from the British Library.

ISBN 1 85793 0851

Printed and bound in Singapore by Tien Wah Press Pte Ltd

2  4  6  8  10  9  7  5  3  1

This book may be ordered by post
direct from the publisher. Please contact
the Marketing Department.
But try your bookshop first.

 here was once a tiger who told the most enormous lies. No matter how hard he tried, he just couldn't tell the truth.

Once the monkey asked the tiger where he was going. The tiger replied that he was on his way to the moon, where he kept a store of tiger-cheese which made his eyes brighter than the sun so that he could see in the dark. But in fact he was going behind a bush for a snooze.

Another time, the snake asked the tiger round for lunch, but the tiger said that he couldn't come because a man had heard him singing in the jungle, and had asked him to go to the big city that very afternoon to sing in the opera.

'Oh!' said the snake. 'Before you go, won't you sing something for me?'

'Ah no,' said the tiger. 'If I sing before I've had my breakfast, my tail swells up and turns into a sausage, and I get followed around by sausage-flies all day.'

One day, all the animals in the jungle held a meeting, and decided they'd cure the tiger of telling such enormous lies. So they sent the monkey off to find the wizard who lived in the snow-capped mountains.

The monkey climbed for seven days and seven nights, and he got higher and higher until at last he reached the cave in the snow where the wizard lived.

At the entrance to the cave he called out: 'Old wizard, are you there?'

And a voice called out: 'Come in, monkey, I've been expecting you.'

So the monkey went into the cave. He found the wizard busy preparing spells, and he told him that the animals of the jungle wanted to cure the tiger of telling such enormous lies.

'Very well,' said the wizard. 'Take this potion and pour it into the tiger's ears when he is asleep.'

'But what will it do, wizard?' asked the monkey.

The wizard smiled and said: 'Rest assured, once you've given him this potion, everything the tiger says will be true all right.'

So the monkey took the potion and went back to the jungle, where he told the other animals what they had to do.

That day, while the tiger was having his usual nap behind the bush, all the other animals gathered round in a circle, and the monkey crept up very cautiously to the tiger and carefully poured a little of the potion first into one of the tiger's ears and then into the other. Then he ran back to the other animals, and they all called out: 'Tiger! Tiger! Wake up, tiger!'

After a while, the tiger opened one eye, and then the other. He was a bit surprised to find all the other animals of the jungle standing around him in a circle.

'Have you been asleep?' asked the lion.

'Oh no,' said the tiger, 'I was just lying here, planning my next expedition to the bottom of the ocean.'

When they heard this, all the other animals shook their heads and said: 'The wizard's potion hasn't worked. Tiger's still telling as whopping lies as ever!'

But just then the tiger found himself leaping to his feet and bounding across the jungle. 'But it's true!' he cried to his own surprise.

'What are you doing, tiger?' they asked.

'I'm going to fly there!' he called and, sure enough, he spread out his legs and soared up high above the trees and across the top of the jungle.

Now if there's one thing tigers don't like, it's heights, and so the tiger yelled out: 'Help! I *am* flying! Get me down!'

But he found himself flying on and on until the jungle was far behind him and he flew over the snow-capped mountains where the wizard lived. The wizard looked up at the tiger flying overhead and smiled to himself and said: 'Ha-ha, old tiger, you'll always tell the truth now. For anything you say will become true – even if it wasn't before!'

And the tiger flew on and on, and he got colder and colder, and if there's one thing tigers hate worse than heights, it's being cold.

At length he found himself flying out over the sea, and then suddenly he dropped like a stone until he came down splash in the middle of the ocean. Now if there's one thing that tigers hate more than heights and cold, it's getting wet.

'Urrrrgh!' said the tiger, but down and down he sank,
right to the bottom of the ocean, and all the fish came up
to him and stared, so he chased them off with his tail.

Then he looked up and he could see the bottom of the waves high above him, and he swam up and up, and just as he was running out of breath, he reached the surface. Then he struggled and splashed and tried to swim for the shore.

Just then a fishing-boat came by, and all the fishermen gasped in amazement to see a tiger swimming in the middle of the ocean. Then one of them laughed and pointed at the tiger and said: 'Look! A sea tiger!'

And they all laughed and pointed at the tiger, and if there's one thing tigers hate worse than heights and cold and getting wet, it's being laughed at.

The poor tiger paddled away as fast as he could, but it was a long way to the shore, and eventually the fishermen threw one of their nets over him and hauled him on to the boat.

'Oh ho!' they laughed. 'Now we can make a fortune by getting this sea tiger to perform tricks in the circus!'

Now this made the tiger really angry, because if there's one thing tigers hate more than heights and cold and getting wet and being laughed at, it's performing tricks in the circus.

So as soon as they landed, he tore up the net, and
leapt out of the boat, and ran home to the forest as fast
as his legs would carry him.

EDUCATION

And he never told any lies, *ever* again.